Dear Reader,

I, Nate the Great, am a detective.
Sometimes I work on cases with
my cousin Olivia Sharp.
She's an Agent for Secrets.
What is an Agent for Secrets?
Olivia will tell you all about it.
She works hard on her cases.
She's here. She's there.
She's everywhere.
She whizzes around the streets
of San Francisco.
Follow her!
I, Nate the Great,
say that you will have
a very good time.

Yours truly,

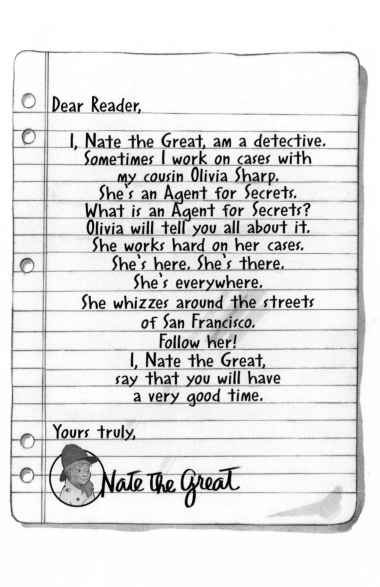

Nate the Great

Olivia Sharp

THE GREEN
TOENAILS GANG

by Marjorie Weinman Sharmat
and Mitchell Sharmat
illustrated by Denise Brunkus

A YEARLING BOOK

Published by
Yearling
an imprint of
Random House Children's Books
a division of Random House, Inc.
New York

Yearling and the jumping horse design are registered trademarks of Random House, Inc.

Visit us on the Web! www.randomhouse.com/kids

Educators and librarians, for a variety of teaching tools, visit us at www.randomhouse.com/teachers

ISBN: 0-440-42063-6 (pbk.)   ISBN: 0-385-90293-X (lib. bdg.)

Reprinted by arrangement with Delacorte Press

Printed in the United States of America

Second Yearling Edition July 2005

10 9 8 7 6 5 4 3 2 1

BVG

FOR A FEW OF THE GOOD FRIENDS
WE'VE CREATED AND LIVED WITH—
NATE THE DETECTIVE, SLUDGE THE
DOG, GREGORY THE GOAT, SHERMAN
THE SLOTH, GENGHIS THE KHAN,
REDDY THE RATTLER, GILA AND
ASSORTED MONSTERS, PHINEAS THE
PIG, MOOCH THE RAT, AND
FANG THE FANG
—M.W.S. AND M.S.

FOR LESLEY
—D.B.

chapter one

My Best Friend

My name is Olivia Sharp.
I'm an agent for secrets.
That means I'm a special
kind of detective.

I'm getting kind of famous in my neighborhood. I work out of an office in my penthouse on top of Pacific Heights in San Francisco.

My best friend is Taffy Plimpton. She used to live in my building on the fourth floor. Not anymore. She moved to Carmel, California. I miss her a lot.

Right after Taffy left I did two things. First I got an owl I named Hoot. Hoot keeps me company, but she's no Taffy Plimpton.

Then I went into the agent-for-secrets business.

chapter two
A Friend in Need

One day I was sitting in my favorite white fluffy chair looking out across San Francisco Bay and smoothing Hoot's feathers. My chauffeur, Willie, came into

4

the room. "A letter for you, Boss,"
he said.

The envelope was postmarked Carmel,
California. I knew the letter was from Taffy.
I tore open the envelope and read:

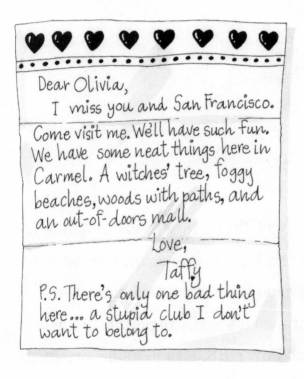

Dear Olivia,
　　I miss you and San Francisco.
Come visit me. We'll have such fun.
We have some neat things here in
Carmel. A witches' tree, foggy
beaches, woods with paths, and
an out-of-doors mall.
　　　　　　　Love,
　　　　　　　　Taffy
P.S. There's only one bad thing
here... a stupid club I don't
want to belong to.

I read Taffy's letter again. Agents for secrets have to know how to read between the lines. That's how they learn what's really important. I knew that Taffy's P.S. was more important than the rest of her letter. It told me that Taffy, secretly, wanted help.

Taffy was in luck. Her best friend is an agent for secrets. I decided to take her case.

chapter three

A Friend Indeed

I went into the kitchen. My housekeeper, Mrs. Fridgeflake, was busy making radishes look like rosebuds.

"I'm going to pop down to Carmel and

visit Taffy Plimpton for the weekend,"
I said.

"Did she invite you?"

"Yes." I showed her Taffy's letter.

"I see she didn't invite Hoot," said Mrs.
Fridgeflake. "That's good. Hoot wouldn't
want to miss the Saturday cartoons.
They're going to show her favorite
tomorrow. *The Owl and the Pussycat.*"

9

Hoot hooted. It was settled.

I went into my office and grabbed my red telephone. It's the one I use for emergency calls.

I called Taffy.

She answered.

I said, "This is Olivia. I got your letter and I'm taking your case. I'm on my way."

I hung up. I never give a client a chance to protest.

Taffy was my first out-of-town client.

I started a file on her:

TAFFY PLIMPTON
OF
CARMEL, CALIFORNIA,
NEEDS ME.

chapter four

Off for the Weekend

I rang for Willie. "We're going to Carmel for the weekend," I said. "Pack fast and bring the limo around."

I stuffed Taffy's file and some clothes

into an overnight bag and dropped a bunch
of my business cards into my pocketbook.

Then I flung my boa over my shoulders,
said good-bye to Hoot and Mrs. Fridgeflake,
and dashed out the door. I took the elevator
to the ground floor.

E.J. was standing in front of the building. He's the boy who moved into Taffy's old apartment.

"Going somewhere, Liver?" he asked.

I do *not* like that nickname!

"The name is Olivia," I said as I stepped

into the limo and slammed the door.

"You said Carmel, Boss?" Willie asked as we rolled out of the courtyard through the iron gates and onto Steiner Street.

"Yes. We're going to Taffy Plimpton's house," I said. "She needs help."

"Life has gotten more interesting since you went into business, Boss," Willie said as he pulled on the visor of his cap.

chapter five

We Arrive

It takes only a couple of hours to drive from San Francisco to Carmel. It's a boring ride with lots of traffic.

I passed the time watching TV and

sipping orange juice in the back of
the limo.

Then I picked up the limo's phone and
called my cousin, Nate the Great, the
detective. I wanted to tell him I was on
my way to my first out-of-town case. But
there wasn't any answer.

So I settled for watching more TV.

It was pretty dark when Willie got us to Taffy's house. He parked the limo in the circular driveway while I ran up the front steps.

I pressed the bell. Chimes rang out.

Taffy flung open the door. She looked just the same. Big eyes. Big freckles. Big smile. And red hair as soft and

fluffy as my boa right after it comes
from the cleaner's.

"Your phone call . . . ," she began.

I said, "You have a problem that you're
trying to keep secret. I'm now an agent
for secrets. Here's my card. I'm also
here as your best friend. I don't have
a card for that."

"It's great that you came," Taffy said.
"But I don't have a secret problem."

I know a problem when I read one.
But I decided it could wait.

I motioned toward my limo. "Willie helps
me with my cases. And my owl, Hoot, gives
me advice. She couldn't make it this weekend. She had other plans."

Taffy gave me a funny look, then
waved to Willie. "Willie can stay in the
guesthouse and you can stay here
with us."

chapter six

Green Toenails

Taffy's mother and father asked a lot of questions.

I told them my parents were in Tibet but they were coming home

next week and I could hardly wait.

I told them that a boy named E.J. had moved into their old apartment. I didn't tell them that he calls me Liver.

After supper Taffy and I took a walk along the beach. Her house overlooks the water. The tide was out. The fog was coming in.

I got down to business.

"I know you want to belong to a club that won't let you in," I said.

Taffy picked up a seashell. "It's a stupid club, just like I wrote you."

"Taffy, darling, lots of clubs are stupid. Like, if three people have green toenails they form a green

toenails club and leave everybody else out."

"Hey, that's a great idea!" Taffy said.

"Let's you and I form a green toenails club and we'll leave everybody else out. We'll be the Green Toenails Gang!"

"Taffy," I said, "how can we be a gang if there are only two of us?"

"Oh."

"I suppose we could ask Willie."

Taffy hugged me. "Terrific. We've got a club. All we need is the green polish."

I knew that this club wouldn't solve Taffy's problem. "When Willie and I go home," I said, "you'll be the only one in town with green toenails and you still won't be a member of the other club."

"Oh."

"Tell me, does this other club have a name?"

"Its name and everything else about it are a secret," Taffy said. "All I know is that each member wears a T-shirt with her first initial on it, printed big."

"Who belongs? What are they like?" I asked.

"There are five members and they all live here in my neighborhood. Millicent, Jasmine, Nettie, Leah, and Katrina. They say they're my friends, but they didn't ask me to join their club." Taffy looked hurt.

That night, before I went to bed, I made a note in my file.

PROBLEM:
THE SECRET FIVE

AIM:
THE SECRET SIX

chapter seven

Those T-shirts

The next morning I had Willie bring the limo around.

"Show me where Millicent, Jasmine, Nettie, Leah, and Katrina live," I said to Taffy.

Taffy gave Willie directions. We started cruising the neighborhood.

Suddenly Taffy cried, "Stop! There they are!"

I saw five girls ahead, riding bicycles. Each girl was wearing a T-shirt with an

initial on it. I immediately knew who each girl was. *M* was for Millicent, *N* was for Nettie, *K* was for Katrina, *L* was for Leah, and *J* was for Jasmine.

"Don't stop," I said to Willie. "Follow those bicycles! Follow those T-shirts!"

"Why?" Taffy asked.

"Isn't it obvious?" I said. "They're a *bicycle* club! Let's see where they're going."

Willie cruised behind the girls. Suddenly he stopped. "Can't go any farther, Boss," he said. "They're going into the woods on a narrow path."

"Wait here," I said.

Taffy and I jumped out of the limo and ran after the bicycle riders. But they were too fast for us.

As we walked back to the limo, I was thinking. *Those girls are too fast for my feet, but they aren't too fast for my head.* I had a plan.

Back in the limo I announced, "We're going to the mall."

chapter eight

Wobble, Tilt, Twist

At the mall I bought a pretty necklace of seashells for Mrs. Fridgeflake. I bought picture postcards for my friends Duncan, Desiree, Sheena, and

Mortimer, and an ankle bracelet
for Hoot.

Then I bought a scented pillow for
Nate the Great. It smelled woodsy and
wonderful. I knew he could use something
like this because he often gets stinky
cases. Two of them landed him in a garbage
pail and the town dump.

But I still couldn't find what I was really
looking for.

"Is there a bicycle shop around here?"
I asked Taffy.

"Down the hill and one street over,"
Taffy said.

At the bicycle store I took out five
hundred dollars and said, "I'll take two
of whatever this buys."

Sometimes it's nice to be rich.

Sometimes it isn't.

This time it was.

We left the shop with the two bikes.

I said, "Here's *your* present, Taffy. Have a bicycle. Either one."

"But I don't know how to ride," Taffy said.

"I know that. I'll teach you. I learned

from a pro last summer on Nantucket
Island."

Taffy and I walked the bikes down the
hill to the bicycle path along Monterey Bay.

Then, with Willie on one side of her and
me on the other, Taffy started her lesson.

Wobble, tilt, twist, wobble, tilt, twist, wobble.

"You can do it," I said.

If you tell someone they can do something, they think you think they can do it, and they never find out that you were just guessing.

It worked.

"Whee! This is fun," Taffy said as Willie and I finally let go.

If I ever have to give up the agent-for-secrets business, maybe I'll become a bike instructor.

chapter nine

Looking Good

Taffy and I headed north on the bicycle path toward Taffy's house. Willie followed with the limo on the road that ran alongside the path.

After we ate lunch, I said, "Now you're ready."

"You know me. I'm always ready," Taffy said. "What am I ready to do this time?"

"To ride your bike in front of the girls. The reason you weren't invited into their club is that you couldn't ride a bicycle."

The first house we rode to was Jasmine's.
We didn't see anybody, and no one
noticed us.

Next stop was at Millicent's.

We were in luck! Millicent was in front
of her house with the other four girls. A
full audience.

Taffy pedaled ahead toward the girls,

shouting, "Look at me!" She screeched to a stop in front of them.

The girls stared at her bike and ran their fingers over it.

Good sign. Taffy was practically a member of the club. This case was practically over.

Taffy beckoned to me.

I pedaled over.

"Olivia," Taffy said, "I want you to meet Jasmine, Nettie, Millicent, Leah, and Katrina."

"Hi," I said.

"Your name is Olivia?" Nettie asked.

"Yes."

Nettie looked at Jasmine, who looked at Millicent, who looked at Katrina, who looked at Leah, who looked at me.

Was there something wrong with my name?

"Where do you live, Olivia?" Katrina asked.

I pointed in the direction of San Francisco. "North of town," I said, and I rode away.

I wanted to leave Taffy alone with the girls. I went back to her house and waited on her front steps.

At last I saw her, bicycling toward me and smiling.

"Quick, tell me," I said. "They asked you to join their club, didn't they?"

"Not yet," Taffy said. "But they invited me to go bike riding with them Monday after school."

"You see?" I said. "That's when they'll invite you to become a member. Remember to act surprised when they

tell you that their secret club is a
bicycle club."

I made a note:

CASE WILL
CLOSE MONDAY.

chapter ten

The Confusing Call

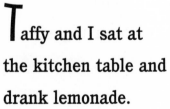

Taffy and I sat at
the kitchen table and
drank lemonade.

The phone rang.

"Maybe it's them and they're
asking me right now," Taffy said.

Taffy grabbed the phone and said hello.

She listened. She looked puzzled.

Then she handed the receiver to me.

"It's for you," she said.

Now *I* was puzzled.

"Hello?"

"Hello, Olivia? This is Nettie. You just met me and my friends, remember?"

"I remember."

"Well, my friends and I have a secret club. Only our members know what the secret is."

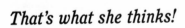

That's what she thinks!

Nettie went on. "Olivia, we knew the moment Taffy introduced you to us that we wanted *you* in our club."

"*Me?*"

"You."

"Why?"

"That's a secret, and I can't tell you our club secret until you join."

"Look," I said, "I already know your secret. You're a bicycle club. It isn't the most original secret, I might add—"

Nettie interrupted. "We're *not* a bicycle club."

I hadn't counted on this.

Nettie pressed on.
"If you join, then
Taffy will be one step
nearer to being asked in.
We like her, but we're not ready for her."

"What do you mean?"

"Can't tell you unless you join. Well . . . ?"

"I'm thinking, I'm thinking."

I hung up.

"Small problem," I said to Taffy. "They
want *me* to join their club."

"They want *you*?" Taffy looked grim. "They don't even know you, and they like you better."

"They don't like me better. Count on it."

I thought about what Nettie had told me. *We knew the moment Taffy introduced you to us that we wanted you in our club.*

Why so fast?

What did they know about me? Taffy told them my name, that's all.

Olivia.

Was there something about *Olivia* that fitted in with their secret?

chapter eleven

What's in a Name?

I wrote down my name in my notebook.
Then I wrote down the girls' names.

Did all the names have something
in common?

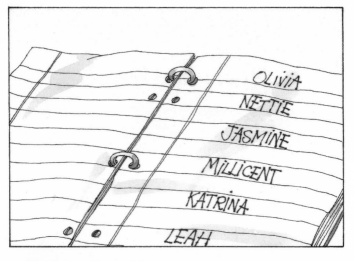

Nothing I could see.

What else did Nettie say?

She said if I joined, then Taffy would be *one step nearer to being asked in.*

What did that mean?

I rewrote the names in a different order.

Nothing clicked.

Something clicked!

I rushed to the door. "I'll be back."

I found Willie in the driveway washing the limo.

"To Jasmine's house," I said.

On the way over I kept thinking, *Now I can help my best friend.*

I rang Jasmine's doorbell. She had
chimes, too.

When she answered, I stepped inside and
made myself comfortable on her couch.

"I know your secret," I said. "*You* probably started this club. Then you invited Katrina to join. Then Leah. Then Millicent. Then Nettie. And now me. You each wear a T-shirt with your first initial on it. *J. K. L. M. N.* And if I join, you'll have an *O.* But Taffy's a *T* and she can't get in until you have a *P, Q, R,* and *S.*"

I started to fluff my boa but then remembered I wasn't wearing it.

"You're an *Alphabet Club!*" I said.

Jasmine gasped.

I said, "I know your secret but you didn't tell me. Therefore, I don't have to keep it."

"Does this mean you're not joining the club?"

"I don't live in Carmel," I said. "I live in San Francisco."

"That's okay. We need an O badly."

I *hate* clubs. All those secret handshakes and pins and meetings and all that rot. And now every time I came down to Carmel I'd be stuck with all that stuff. But I had to join. I had to give them an O.

"I'll join," I said, "if you invite Taffy in. What good is a club that makes somebody feel left out and unhappy?"

"Taffy will get in," Jasmine said. "But it'll take time."

I stood up. I put my hands on my hips. *"Rush it!"* I said.

Jasmine looked blank.

I, an agent for secrets, knew how to rush it.
I opened my pocketbook, fished out one
of my cards, and scribbled something on it.

I underlined five letters and gave the card to Jasmine. "Read this carefully," I said, "and get back to us. I'll keep your secret for twenty-four hours."

Jasmine looked at my card. "I'll see what I can do," she said.

chapter twelve

Wait and See

Willie drove me back to Taffy's.

She was waiting for me. "What's up?" she asked.

"Wait and see," I said. "Trust me."

The next day Taffy
and I went to the
Witches' Tree and
had a picnic lunch
under it.

We went for a walk in
the woods.

We watched the
fog gather over the
Pacific Ocean.

Then I packed to go home.

I looked at my
watch. The
twenty-four hours
were almost up.

The telephone rang.

"It's for you this time," I said.

Taffy picked up the receiver.

She said the following:

"Hello." (Pause)

"Really?" (Pause)

"Yes!" (Pause)

"What?" (Pause)

"Well, I'll get used

to it." (Pause)

"Bye." (Pause)

She hung up. She shouted, "It was Jasmine. She asked me into the club and I said yes!"

Success!

"They're going to tell me their secret at the next meeting."

I hugged Taffy. "Aren't you glad we didn't start the Green Toenails Gang?"

"You bet," Taffy said.

I picked up my overnight bag.

"Just one thing," Taffy said. "Jasmine called me Plimp. Isn't that a silly nickname?"

"No, I rather like it," I said.

chapter thirteen

Homeward Bound

My visit was over. My client was happy. Now all I had to do was go home and face E.J. and my own nickname.

Willie brought the limo around.

"So long, best friend," Taffy said.

"So long, Plimp," I said.

Willie started the limo and we rolled out
of the circular driveway.

I pulled my file on the case.

I wrote:

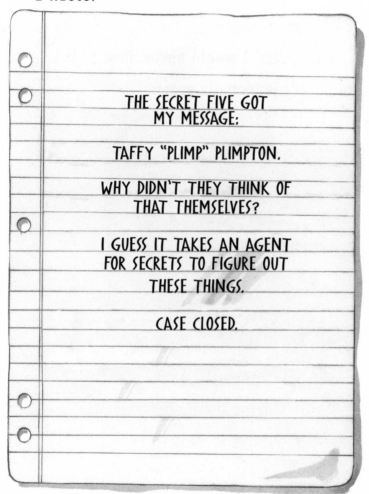

THE SECRET FIVE GOT
MY MESSAGE:

TAFFY "PLIMP" PLIMPTON.

WHY DIDN'T THEY THINK OF
THAT THEMSELVES?

I GUESS IT TAKES AN AGENT
FOR SECRETS TO FIGURE OUT
THESE THINGS.

CASE CLOSED.

The fog was creeping in.

Willie turned north, and we drove toward San Francisco.

I was glad I would never have to ask him to paint his toenails green.